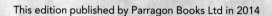

For L and G
"Fly high"
– H.F.

This edition published by Parragon Books Ltd in 2014

Parragon Books Ltd
Chartist House
15–17 Trim Street
Bath BA1 1HA, UK
www.parragon.com

Written by Margaret Wise Brown
Illustrated by Henry Fisher

Edited by Laura Baker
Designed by Ailsa Cullen
Production by Emma Fulleylove

ISBN 978-1-4723-0786-6

Printed in China

Away
in my Aeroplane

PaRragon

Bath • New York • Cologne • Melbourne • Delhi
Hong Kong • Shenzhen • Singapore • Amsterdam

Riding along in my

aeroplane,

and through the rain.

Riding along in my aeroplane,
Sometimes I meet a bird
way up high in the sky,

Flying almost as fast as I fly –

But not as high!

Riding along
in my aeroplane,

Out of the sunlight and

Then out of the clouds

and sun again,

Riding along in my aeroplane!

Down below the people go,
very small and very slow.

They look like bugs and ants and flies—
I wonder if they realize
What they look like to my eyes.

Riding along in my aeroplane,

I dash straight up in the air
And wheel about.

I plunge through the sunlight,

Then I glide

down to the earth

in my aeroplane.

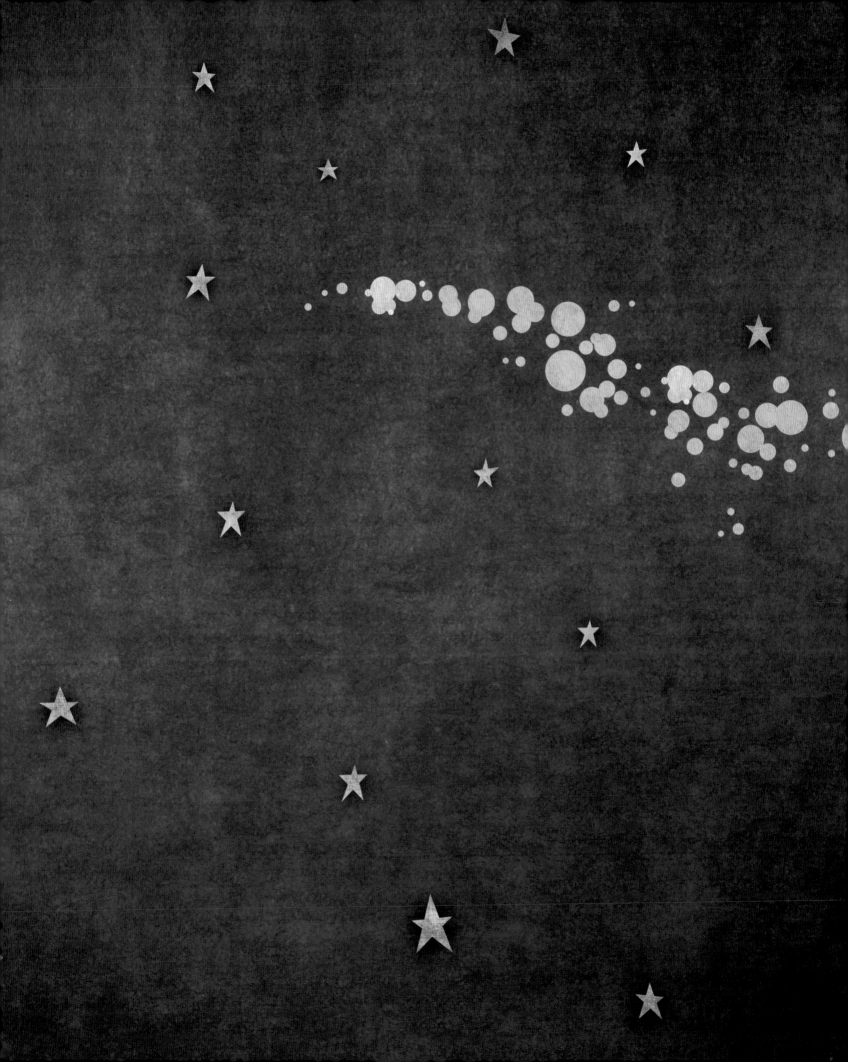